Book Club Edition
 Published in the United States by Random House, Inc., New York, and simultaneously in Canada by Random House of Canada Limited, Toronto. Originally published in Denmark as TIM OG BUM NARRER KATTEN LUCIFER by Gutenberghus Gruppen, Copenhagen.
ISBN: 0-394-84807-1
Manufactured in the United States of America
4 5 6 7 8 9 0 B C D E F G H I J K

How Cinderella's Mice Tricked Lucifer the Cat

Random House New York

Cinderella lived with her stepmother and her stepsisters.

They made her do all the housework.

She had to scrub the floors every day.

She had to wash the dishes
after every meal.

Her stepsisters never did any work.

They just gave orders.

"Wash my dress! Make my bed!" they ordered Cinderella.

"Clean that floor better!" said her stepmother.
Everyone scolded poor Cinderella for something.
She could not please ANYONE.

Cinderella was unhappy.
She worked so hard.
And she had no one to talk to.

When Cinderella had finished her chores,
she would go to the attic.

Her bed was in the attic.

Lucifer the sly cat
would follow Cinderella
up the stairs.

But Cinderella would never let Lucifer in the attic.

He liked to chase the mice who lived there.

"Your home is downstairs," Cinderella would say to Lucifer.

The attic was small and filled with junk.

But Cinderella had made her part of it very cozy.

She loved to sit by the window.

Cinderella always fed the birds. They liked to eat breadcrumbs from her hand.

There were lots of mice in the attic.
Cinderella fed them, too.

Cinderella sewed little dresses and shirts for the mice.

They were her friends.

And she would tell them bedtime stories.

She always warned the mice to watch out for Lucifer the cat.

He just loved to chase mice!

But one night Gus and Jack, two hungry mice, went in search of a piece of cheese.

They tiptoed down the stairs.

They crept into the kitchen.
"The coast is clear!" whispered Gus.

They could smell
the cheese.

There it was.
What a big chunk of cheese!
Gus and Jack were ready to take a piece.
They did not see Lucifer hiding.

All of a sudden Lucifer leaped onto the table.

Everything fell with a clatter!

Then the cat began to chase the hungry mice.

"Hurry Gus!" squealed Jack. "Just a few more stairs to go!"

"Meow!" cried Lucifer. He was hungry too!

WHEW!

The mice ran into their mouse hole just in time.

Lucifer was very unhappy.

“We’re safe!” sighed Jack.

All the mice ran over to them.

Grandma Mouse spoke first. "This must stop. Cinderella is right. We have to be more careful. That cat is very bad."

Just then the youngest mouse brought out a bell with a long ribbon.

"Let's tie this to Lucifer's tail," he said.

"Good idea," said Jack. "Then we'll always hear him."

Grandma Mouse told them how to do it.

Gus and Jack began to follow Grandma's plan.
Quietly they carried the bell to the kitchen.

But...
OOPS!
Gus tripped!
The bell tinkled....

And mean old Lucifer woke up!

“I’ll get them now!” said Lucifer.
He ran right after them.

Once again, Gus and Jack ran for their lives!

And once again, they made it home safely!
But they were all worn out.

"We must make another plan,"
Grandma Mouse decided.

Just then the birds came to visit.
The mice told the birds their problem.
The birds chirped for a minute.
"We have an idea," they said.

"Tomorrow is Lucifer's birthday," said the birds. "We will give him the bell and the ribbon as a gift. The bell is very pretty. He will want to wear it right away. He will not know that he is being tricked!"

So the mice began
to wrap the bell at once.

How beautiful the box looked!
"It is a shame this is for that cat," said Grandma Mouse.

"How will we get the box to Lucifer's party?" asked Grandma Mouse.

"We will take it there," said the birds.

The next morning, the stepmother, the stepsisters, and Cinderella gave Lucifer his gifts.

Cinderella knew which gift belonged to the mice.

But she did not tell whom the gift was from.

Cinderella unwrapped the gift for Lucifer.

She clapped for joy when she saw the bell.

How smart those mice are, she thought.

"Lucifer, look at this pretty bell and ribbon," she said. "I will make a beautiful bow for you!"

Lucifer purred with joy.

The plan worked.

Lucifer never knew that the mice could hear the bell.

All he thought of was how good he looked.

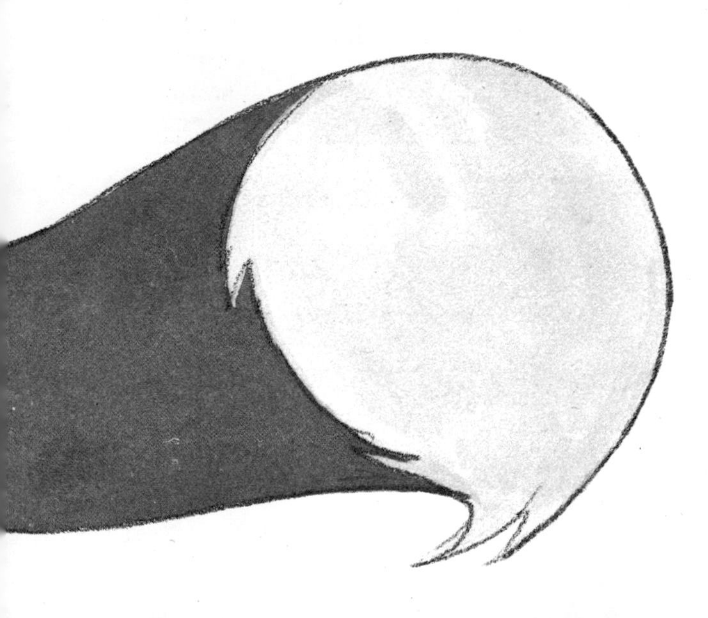

In fact, the stepmother and stepsisters had a portrait made of Lucifer wearing his bell!

They thought he looked *very* handsome.

So the mice always heard the bell ring when Lucifer was near.

And they always had enough time to run away from that silly old cat!